OF THE
UNIVERSE

Raid of the Alien Mice

Adapted by Robin Snyder
Designed by Deborah Bethel

PlayValue Books™
A Division of Grosset & Dunlap

* ™ & © 1984, 1985 World Events Productions, Ltd. All rights reserved. Licensed by Merchandising Corporation of America, Inc. PlayValue Books is a trademark of The Putnam Publishing Group. Published by PlayValue Books™, a division of Grosset & Dunlap, a member of The Putnam Publishing Group, New York. Published simultaneously in Canada. Printed in Italy. ISBN 0-448-81890-6   B C D E F G H I J

One lovely evening in The Castle of Lions, Princess Allura and her mouse, Cheddar, watched what they believed to be falling stars.

They both made wishes. Allura wished for peace on Planet Arus. Cheddar, naturally, wished for cheese.

Unknown to the princess, however, these were not simply falling stars.

They were actually dangerous creatures sent by the terrible witch, Haggar.

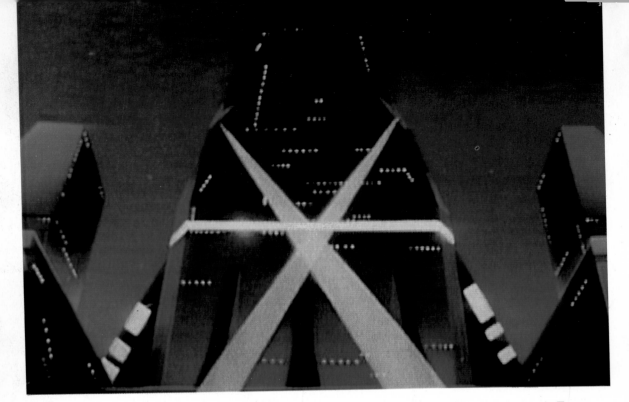

Suddenly, the alarm went off at Castle Control, awakening the Voltron Force.

"Have we got trouble?" asked Keith, the leader of Voltron Force.

"There's an alarm, but I don't see a problem!" responded Coran, counselor to Lion Force.

The team was baffled, but little Cheddar soon discovered the reason for the alarm.

Meanwhile, fire broke out in the computer's electrical system!

Everyone at Castle Control raced to put out the fire.

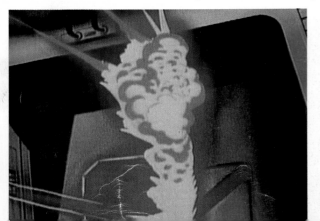

Soon the fire was brought under control. The Voltron Force gathered to investigate. "We'd better check for damage on the monitor," suggested Coran.

"A hole chewed in metal?" said Princess Allura. "What could have caused that?"

"Let's take a look around," said Keith.

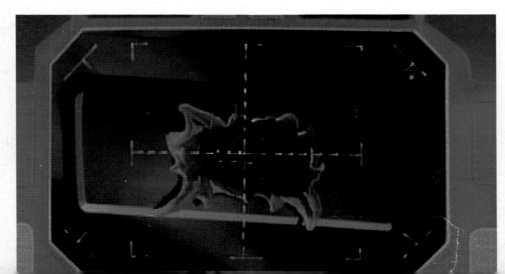

They soon found the cause of all the trouble.

"Killer mice!" exclaimed Keith. "They can shoot deadly beams from their eyes!"

"Look!" he continued. "They damaged the computer's electrical system. That must have started the fire!"

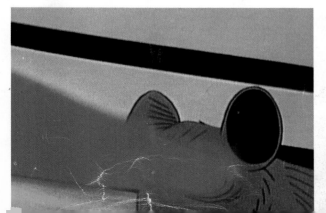

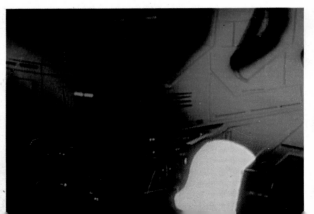

Meanwhile in evil King Zarkon's castle, the horrible witch, Haggar, saw all this in her crystal ball. "My darling little rodents are paralyzing the castle's computer system. While Planet Arus is in a weakened condition, we will send our mighty Robeast to finish them off!" the old witch cackled.

Back at Castle Control, the robot alien mice continued their evil work.

They cut the power to the castle's view-screen...

...and headed for the main computer!

"If they reach the main computer, the whole castle will be shut down!" worried Coran.

Brave little Cheddar had a plan. Having outrun the killer mice earlier, he now volunteered to lead them into a trap.

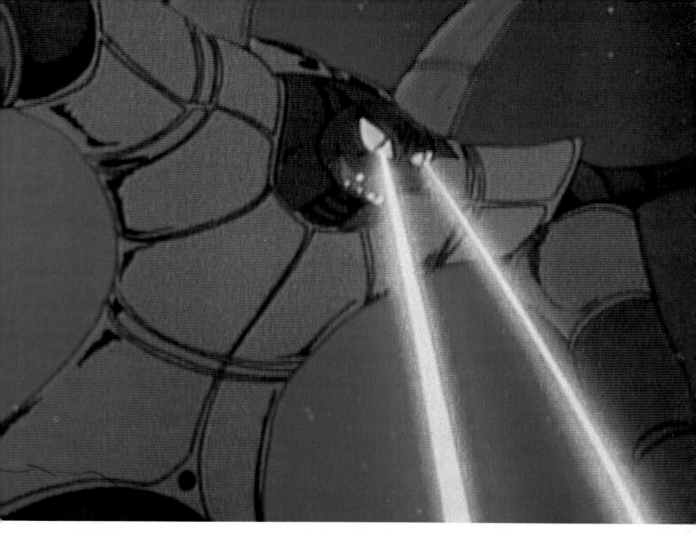

Cheddar ran off, just as a tremendous roar came from outside. Haggar's mighty Robeast had arrived!

Keith began shouting orders. "Princess, Pidge, guard that computer. Lance, Hunk, we've got to get to the Lions!"

The alien mice had knocked out the solar generator, so there wasn't enough power to drive to the Lions. The three friends had to run to their Lions to try to stop the attack of the Robeast.

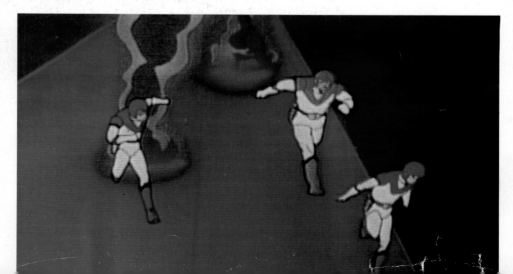

While Keith, Lance, and Hunk ran for their Lions, Cheddar confronted the robot alien mice.

He taunted them…   …made them chase him…

…and led them into…   …a deadly trap!

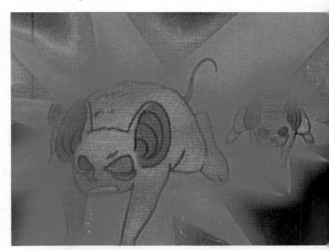

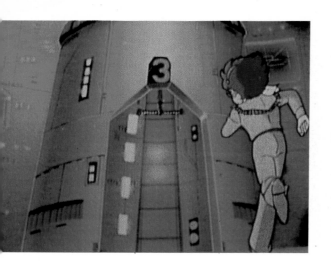
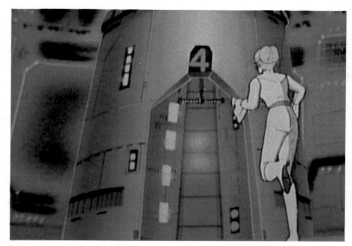

With the alien mice destroyed, and the castle's computers working again, Pidge and the princess rushed to their Lions.

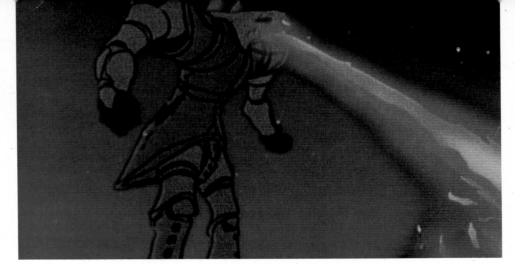

Meanwhile, the Robeast started a fire in the woods!

Lance, Hunk, and Keith were trapped. "We're caught!" exclaimed Hunk. "You know it," said Lance. "Fire ahead of us, and Robeast behind!"

Out of the sky roared the Green and Blue Lions, spraying water to put out the fire!

"Quick, grab on to the claw," said the princess.
Keith, Hunk, and Lance jumped on board, and were quickly brought to their own Lions.

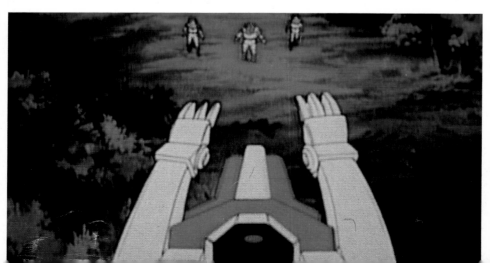

But even the power of all five Lions was not enough to stop the powerful Robeast. "There's only one thing to do!" shouted Keith. "Ready to form Voltron!"

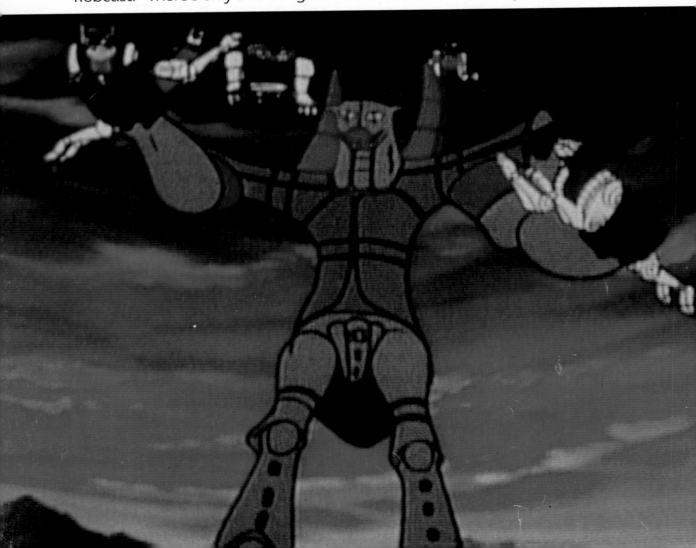

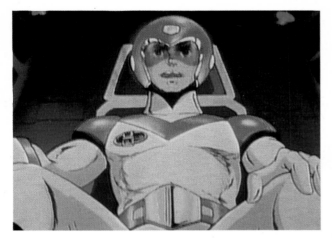

"Activate Interlocks...
Dynotherms connected...
Infracells up...Megathrusters
are go," ordered Keith.

"Let's go Voltron Force!"
all five said together.

"Form feet and legs!" said Keith.

"Form arms and body!" he continued.

The Lion Robots had formed the mightiest warrior in history: VOLTRON —DEFENDER OF THE UNIVERSE!

"And I'll form the head!" he finished.

"O.K. team!" said Keith. "It's time for this Robeast to go down!"

With a mighty surge of strength, Voltron smashed the evil creature to the ground.

"Now, let's finish him!" shouted the team leader. "Form Blazing Sword!"

Like a hot knife through butter, Voltron's Blazing Sword ripped through the mechanical body of the Robeast!

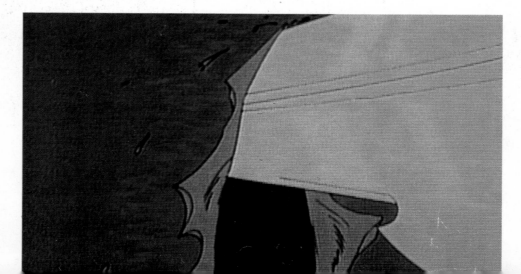

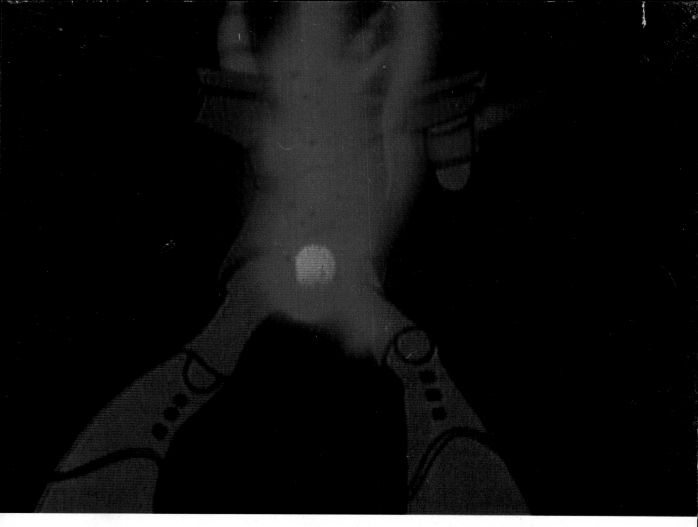

"Another one of Zarkon's 'toys' to the scrap metal heap!" said Hunk, with a smile, as the Robeast exploded and collapsed.

Later, back at Castle Control, Cheddar's wish for some cheese, finally came true.

As for the princess' wish for peace, at least for tonight, all was safe on Arus, thanks to VOLTRON—DEFENDER OF THE UNIVERSE.